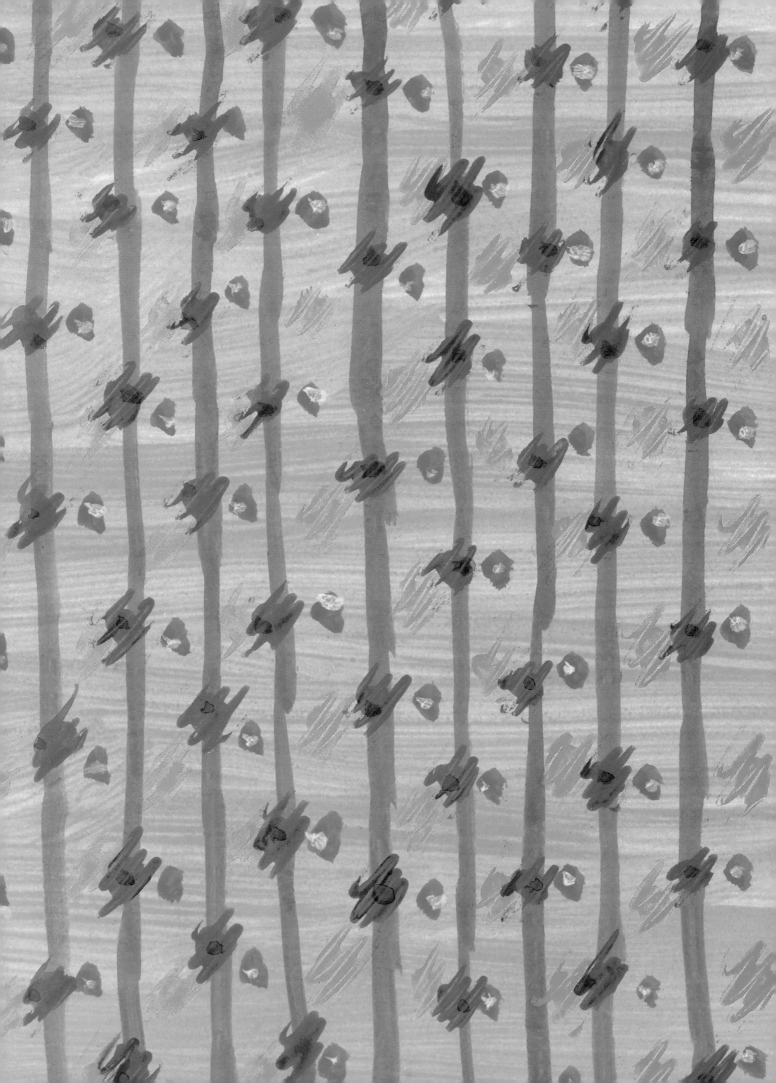

For
Susan,
Hubert
&
Andrzej

Today Is Monday Pictures by **Eric Carle**

PAPERSTAR

Penguin Young Readers Group

Today Is Monday
Monday, string beans

Tuesday, spaghetti
Monday, string beans

Wednesday, ZOOOOP
Tuesday, spaghetti
Monday, string beans

Thursday, roast beef
Wednesday, ZOOOOP
Tuesday, spaghetti
Monday, string beans

Friday, fresh fish
   Thursday, roast beef
   Wednesday, ZOOOOP
   Tuesday, spaghetti
   Monday, string beans

Saturday, chicken
Friday, fresh fish
Thursday, roast beef
Wednesday, ZOOOOP
Tuesday, spaghetti
Monday, string beans

Sunday, ice cream
Saturday, chicken
Friday, fresh fish
Thursday, roast beef
Wednesday, ZOOOOP
Tuesday, spaghetti
Monday, string beans

All you hungry children
Come and eat it up!

Today Is Monday

To - day is Mon - day, ____ to - day is Mon - day,

Mon - day string beans, All you hun - gry chil - dren,

Come and eat it up. To - day is Tues - day, _ to - day is Tues - day,

Tues - day spa - ghet - ti, Mon - day string beans, All you hun - gry chil - dren

Come and eat it up. To - day is Come and eat it up. ____

Today is Monday, today is Monday
Monday, string beans
All you hungry children
Come and eat it up.

Today is Tuesday, today is Tuesday
Tuesday, spaghetti
Monday, string beans
All you hungry children
Come and eat it up.

Today is Wednesday, today is Wednesday
Wednesday, ZOOOOP
Tuesday, spaghetti
Monday, string beans
All you hungry children
Come and eat it up.

Today is Thursday, today is Thursday
Thursday, roast beef
Wednesday, ZOOOOP
Tuesday, spaghetti
Monday, string beans
All you hungry children
Come and eat it up.

Today is Friday, today is Friday
Friday, fresh fish
Thursday, roast beef
Wednesday, ZOOOOP
Tuesday, spaghetti
Monday, string beans
All you hungry children
Come and eat it up.

Today is Saturday, today is Saturday
Saturday, chicken
Friday, fresh fish
Thursday, roast beef
Wednesday, ZOOOOP
Tuesday, spaghetti
Monday, string beans
All you hungry children
Come and eat it up.

Today is Sunday, today is Sunday
Sunday, ice cream
Saturday, chicken
Friday, fresh fish
Thursday, roast beef
Wednesday, ZOOOOP
Tuesday, spaghetti
Monday, string beans
All you hungry children
Come and eat it up.

Eric Carle prepares his own colored tissue papers. Different textures are achieved by
using various brushes to splash, spatter and finger paint acrylic paints onto thin tissue papers.
These colored tissue papers then become his palette. They are cut or torn into shapes as needed
and are glued onto white illustration board. Some areas of his designs, however, are painted directly on the board
before the bits of paper are applied to make the collage illustrations.
The art is then scanned by laser and reproduced in full color.

Library of Congress Cataloging-in-Publication Data
Carle, Eric. Today is Monday/by Eric Carle. p. cm. Summary: Each day of the week brings
a new food, until on Sunday all the world's children can come and eat it up. Children's songs—Texts.
[1. Food—Songs and music. 2. Songs.] I. Title. PZ8.3.C1945To 1993
782.42164'0268—dc20 91-45866 CIP AC ISBN 978-0-698-11563-7

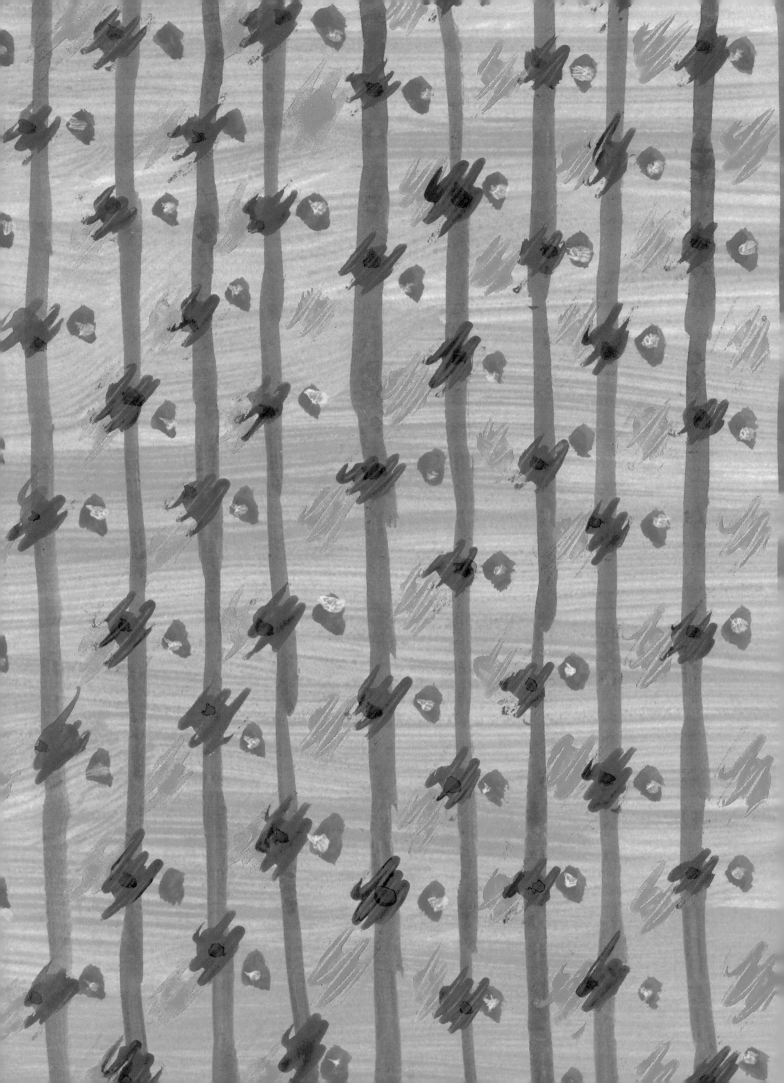

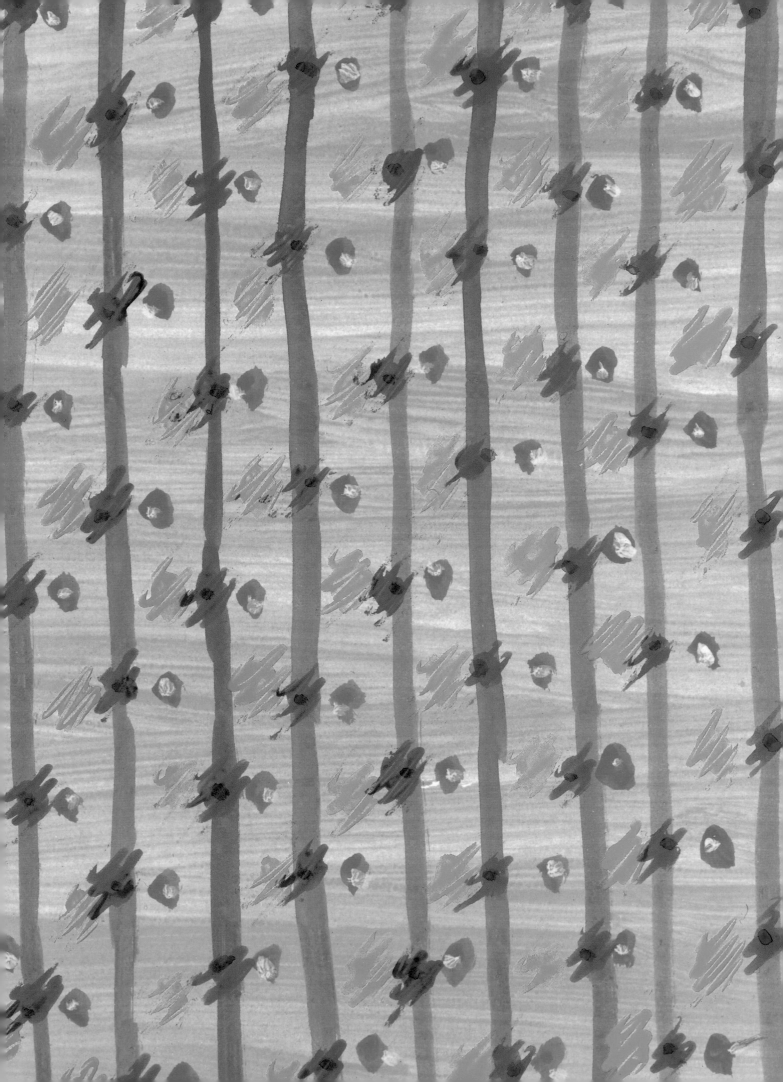